ISBN 0 340 14783 0

Copyright © 1969 Gunilla Wolde
SAGA/Läromedelsförlagen
English text copyright © 1970 Brockhampton Press Ltd
(now Hodder and Stoughton Children's Books)

First published in Great Britain 1970
This impression 1989

Published by Hodder and Stoughton Children's Books,
a division of Hodder and Stoughton Ltd,
Mill Road, Dunton Green, Sevenoaks, Kent TN13 2YJ

Printed in Great Britain by Purnell and Sons (Book Production) Ltd,
Member of BPCC plc, Paulton, Bristol

Co-edition arranged with the help of Angus Hudson, London

All rights reserved

Gunilla Wolde

THOMAS
goes out

English text
Alison Winn

HODDER AND STOUGHTON
LONDON SYDNEY AUCKLAND TORONTO

The moment Thomas gets up in the morning he wants to go out and play. Mother says, "It's very cold outside, Thomas. You must put on some warm clothes first."

Thomas has a
lot of warm clothes.
He wonders which to put on.

He starts with his furry winter hat with the floppy ear flaps.

And his red woolly jersey.
His jersey seems to have
shrunk. He can't get it on
over his head.

So he pulls off his jersey
and pulls off his hat,
and starts all over again.

This time he puts on his
jersey first and his hat next.
"That's better," says Thomas.

"Now I shall put on
my waterproof jacket."

He has fun sliding the zipper
up and down, up and down.

"Next," says Thomas,
"I'll put on my long
green trousers."

"That can't be right," says Thomas, as ten pink toes peep out of one trouser leg.

So he takes off his long
green trousers and his
blue waterproof jacket,
and starts all over again.

"Now I shall put on my tights,"
says Thomas.
"Tights are funny things, the more
you pull the longer they grow."

"Look, there's a lot left over
with no more inside,"
says Thomas.
"I've got funny feet,
funny feet, funny feet."
He sings and dances
a little jig.

Now Thomas
finds his mittens.

But puts them on his feet
instead of his hands.

Then he takes his mittens off his feet
and puts on his warm yellow socks.

Is he ready now?

No, he's forgotten
his long green trousers.

He gets them on the right way this time but one button is missing.

So his trousers
keep slipping down.

Until he gets on his
blue waterproof jacket.

"Now," says Thomas,
"all I need is my blue wellington boots."
And he takes a flying leap
into them.

At last Thomas
is ready to go out.

He has on
  his boots
  his trousers
  his tights
  his socks
  his jersey
  his jacket
  his mittens
  and his furry winter hat
  with the floppy ear flaps.